FLYBOY OF UNDERWHERE

by **BRUCE HALE**

illustrated by
SHANE HILLMAN

HarperTrophy®
An Imprint of HarperCollinsPublishers

Flyboy of Underwhere
Text copyright © 2008 by Bruce Hale
Illustrations copyright © 2008 by Shane Hillman
All rights reserved. Printed in the United States of America. No part of this book
may be used or reproduced in any manner whatsoever without written per-
mission except in the case of brief quotations embodied in critical articles and
reviews. For information address HarperCollins Children's Books, a division of
HarperCollins Publishers, 1350 Avenue of the Americas, New York, NY 10019.
www.harpercollinschildrens.com

Library of Congress Catalog Card Number: 2008020221
ISBN 978-0-06-085132-3

Typography by Jennifer Heuer
09 10 11 12 13 LP/CW 10 9 8 7 6 5 4 3 2 1
❖
First Harper Trophy edition, 2009

To Miguelito—
smooth sailing,
my friend

FLYBOY of UNDERWHERE

Chasing Melvin

Everybody wants to be the hero; nobody wants to be the sidekick. It's true. Ask any two kids playing Batman and Robin, or Sherlock Holmes and Dr. Watson. Nobody wants to be Robin.

And the doctor? Forget about it.

(It's not just the dorky costume, either. Heroes get to be cool. Sidekicks get to tell the hero how cool *he* is.)

That's my problem. I don't want to be the sidekick. But sometimes I feel like I'm not even the hero of my *own* life.

If you've heard about our adventures from my

buddy Zeke and his twin sister, Stephanie, you'll know that he's the Lost Prince of Underwhere (the place, not the cottony-fresh stuff you're wearing under your clothes). And Stephanie? She's the Lost Princess.

What am *I*? The Lost Cheese Wrangler, the Lost Beebee Stacker, the Lost Whatchamadingy.

It's my own fault. I just can't make up my mind about some stuff. And a hero should be able to make up his mind, right?

It's like that guy, Hamlet, said: "To be or not to be . . . something."

Let me explain.

My story starts with me nosing through the construction site, searching for Fitz, my talking orange cat. (He meows, sure, but he also talks English. More on that later.) Then I spotted something that looked like trouble.

Some*one*, actually.

Melvin Prang, school bully, was slipping into the secret passage to Underwhere, carrying a mysterious bag. Since Steph, Zeke, and I have been fighting to free Underwhere from the dirty rotten UnderLord and his pet zombies, this worried me.

Underwhere didn't need another bully.

Just then, Fitz turned up.

"*Mwrr reer eerow,*" he said in his weird cat talk, jerking his head toward the sidewalk. He's been chatty ever since this Throne that looks like a fancy toilet came to Zeke and Steph's house. (More on that later too.)

I figured he meant we should go get my friends. Fitz smelled them coming up the street before I saw them. (Which doesn't mean that they're stinky, really—just that Fitz has a keen nose.)

"Hey, guys!" I dashed over and told them what I'd seen.

"Melvin's in Underwhere?!" cried Steph.

"Actually, he's *always* in underwear," said Zeke. "I'm guessing boxers."

"Real funny." Steph's jaw tightened. "Melvin could cause some serious damage down there!"

"What should we do?" I said.

"Duh, Hector—go after him," Steph said. She began pulling her curly brown hair into a ponytail.

"No time for primping, Stephasaurus," said Zeke.

Her chin went up. "I'm not sliding down that filthy tube without some basic preparations."

Fitz batted at my leg. *"Reer mmrow!"*

I knew how he felt. Waving my hand between them, I said, "Uh, guys? About Melvin—"

Zeke made a face. "Aw, hush!"

"Don't shush me," I said.

"No." He pointed past my shoulder. "The guys from H.U.S.H."

Steph winced.

Fitz hissed.

I turned. *Yikes.*

Two men were getting out of a silver car. They wore identical black suits and dark sunglasses. They might just as well have had GOVERNMENT AGENT stamped across their foreheads, except their foreheads were covered by two really phony-looking wigs.

"Hold it!" cried the tall one with blond surfer hair. Unfortunately the wig didn't hide a honking great mole on his cheek. That mole had its own zip code.

Zeke, Steph, and I exchanged a look. The spies were between us and the construction site.

What to do?

"Now, children," said the chubby one from under a mop of red clown curls. "We've got a bone to pick with you."

Zeke put up a hand. "Can't you pick it later? We've got to be somewhere."

Agent Mole planted himself in front of us and rumbled, "Sure do. Right here."

"Sheesh," said Zeke.

Agent Belly crossed his arms. "What's the big idea, giving us a painted toilet brush instead of a magic gizmo?"

"We never!" I said. Actually, we *had*—only a couple of days earlier.

Steph pulled her big-eyed innocent face. "What are you talking about?" She's pretty good at lying for someone who never practices.

"You know perfectly well," said the chubby spy. "Thanks to you three, your government wasted a week running tests on a toilet brush that you swore was some Brush of Wisdom from your 'Under-land.' We were disappointed and, urr, none the wiser."

"Disappointed," said Mole. His scowl was mean. It probably would've been meaner if he hadn't had to blow long, fake hairs away from his mouth.

"But the bathrooms did sparkle," Belly said to Mole. Mole grunted.

Steph held up her palms. "Honestly, we thought it was the real thing."

"That's right," said Zeke. "Somebody must have pulled a switch on us."

"*Sure*," said Agent Mole. "And you have no idea who."

Actually, we knew exactly who had swapped the brushes: our school custodian, Mr. Wheener.

Maybe if I told them, we could give these guys the brush-off.

"You should check out Mr. Wheener at our school," I said. "He's been acting suspicious."

Agent Belly tossed his curls. "Wrong," he said. "*You* should check out Wheener."

"But *you're* the spies," I said.

The chubby agent leaned toward me. "Don't get smart. Investigate this Wheener and bring us a *real* magical artifact, or . . . your grandmother might get deported."

"But she's a U.S. citizen!" cried Stephanie.

"Oh," said Belly. "Then your landlord might kick you out."

"But they own their house," said Zeke.

Agent Belly frowned. "Then your, uh . . . cat might choke on a giant hairball."

"*Wurrr, meer roor reauwww,*" Fitz muttered.

I picked him up. "Stay away from Fitz."

"Give us what we want, and the pussycat will be fine." Agent Belly reached out to pat Fitz, who swiped his claws at the man.

Belly jumped back, and Agent Mole struck

8

a kung fu pose. "Bad kitty!"

Hiding behind his partner, Agent Belly straightened his wig. "Let's see some results, children!" He backed toward the car. "Or things will get rough."

And with a last glare at Fitz, they departed.

"Is it just me," I said, "or do they leave a bad taste in your mouth?"

Zeke sniffed. "Judging by your breath, there *is* a bad taste in your mouth. But those guys bug me, too."

"Can we go now?" said Steph.

We hustled over to the construction site gate and squeezed through.

The rotten-egg smell grew stronger. We entered a corner room with a dark hole in the middle of the floor. A strong breeze seemed to pull us closer.

"I'd hate to say this place sucks," I said.

"But if the shoe fits . . ." said Zeke.

Steph shook her head. "Honestly, you two."

And with that, we stepped forward and dropped down to Underwhere.

CHAPTER 2

WHAT AM I, LASSIE? I DON'T KNOW YOUR FRIEND'S SMELL.

SOMETHING TELLS ME MELVIN WAS HERE.

WHAT?

THAT.

MELVIN RULEZ!!!

SHH! WHAT'S THAT SOUND?

AAAAAHHHH!

ZOMBIES! FLEE!

WHAT'S THE RUSH? ZOMBIES ARE SLOW.

UH, GUYS?

YEAH?

NOT *THESE* ZOMBIES!

HEY! THE ZOMBIES HAVE SKATES!

WE NOTICED.

SO WHY ARE WE RUNNING DOWN THE ROAD?

DUH!

WHERE IN THE WORLD DID ZOMBIES GET ROLLERBLADES?

WHERE ELSE? FROM OUR WORLD.

MELVIN.

THAT'S WHAT WAS IN HIS BAG.

UNNGH!!!

POUNCE!

UNGHH!

PEGASUS!?

OH, JOY. SOMEONE REMEMBERS MY NAME.

WOOOSH!

GNARRR!!

BOP! BAP!

THEY WON'T LET GO OF MY CLOTHES!

THEN STRIP!

WHAT?!

IT'S YOUR ONLY CHANCE!

ZIP!

AAAH!

GNRFF?

GNEEE!

DON'T MIND ME. I'M JUST PEACHY!

THAT WAS A CLOSE CALL.

CLOTHES CALL IS MORE LIKE IT! HA!

WOOSH

NOW, WHERE WERE WE?

LOOKING FOR MELVIN.

UH-UH. WE'RE GOING HOME FOR CLOTHES.

CLOTHES? I THINK I SAW SOMETHING...

CHECK IT OUT.

ALL HAIL, HOLY FLEECIES

ALL HAIL, HOLY

THANKS, FITZ! JUST WHAT I, UH, NEED...

3

Undercover Cat

Pip-pip-pop-pop! We shot out of the hole and landed, a heap of kids and cat. Underwhere would have to put up with Melvin a little longer. We had a quest.

First stop: Zeke and Steph's house, to borrow me some clothes. A guy can't just run around the streets in his holy fleecies, even if it *does* make him look like an Undie warrior.

We burst through the door and hit our first obstacle: Cousin Caitlyn.

"Where have you zimwats been?" she said. "I've been, like, totally frazzing over here. Did it slip your teeny-weeny minds that you promised to help make dinner tonight?"

That's Caitlyn. All college student, all mouth. She's babysitting Zeke and Steph while their parents are off at a dig.

"Uh, no," said Zeke. "We didn't forget."

Caitlyn crossed her arms. "So you mean you null noggins are late *on purpose*?"

"That's not what he meant," Steph said.

"Whatever," said Caitlyn, grabbing them by the elbows. "You can flap your fish lips and tell me all about it while you peel spudskies."

"But we—" I said.

For the first time, she noticed me. "Nice getup, Hector. Hey, your old grans called. She said to get your fun-bucket home *now*."

"But we've gotta—" Zeke said.

"Make up for being late?" said Caitlyn. "Aw, that's sweet, dinky doodle. And you *will*. Now, march!"

She shoved me out the door and—*bam!*—slammed it shut.

There I was, a kid in his underwear, on his neighbor's steps.

I looked up and down the street. A lady in a passing car gawked. A man watering his yard stared and snickered.

In this situation, there's only one thing a guy like me can do: Run like heck.

On the way to school the next day, we hatched our plans.

"But we can't just hang out and spy on Mr. Wheener," said Stephanie.

"Why not?" I asked as we headed down the sidewalk.

She spread her hands. "Because," she said, "he knows we know he knows something about the Brush, and we know he knows we want it. You know?"

"No," said Zeke.

"No?" said Steph.

I bent to pet Fitz.

"*Mrrrrrr,*" he purred.

Steph fiddled with her curls. "Then what do you suggest? Play in the halls near his office and hope to catch him with it? He'll spot us in a second."

Fitz wound around my ankles. I smiled as an idea came. "Who said anything about *us* spying?" I said, looking down at my cat.

He gazed up with big golden eyes. "*Wurr meer?*"

"Fitzie?" said Steph.

I smiled. "He'd be perfect. Who would suspect a cat?"

Fitz shook his head in disgust.

"Come on, Fitz," said Zeke.

Steph squatted beside Fitz and scratched behind his ear, in that spot that turns him to jelly. "Pleeeease?"

Fitz shook his head no. *"Murr! Meeer wurr rowr . . ."* But as Stephanie continued to scratch, he melted into a furry, purring blob.

That settled, we walked to school and split up for our classes.

My teacher, Mr. Manju, greeted us with a smile. "Good morning, everyone!"

"'Mawning, Mistuh Monjuh," we mumbled. That man is *way* too cheerful in the early hours.

"Your Career Reports are due next week. Let's go around the room and check in!"

I ducked my head.

Whoops. Once again, I hadn't made up my mind.

I'd actually known about the assignment for a week. We each had to research a job and do a presentation on it. Simple, right?

Just one problem: I hadn't actually picked a career.

Down the line it went, each kid sounding off. *Artist. Scientist. Teacher. Rock star.* They made it sound so sure, so easy.

Then it was my turn.

"Uh, well . . ." I said.

Mr. Manju nodded. "Yes, Hector?"

"Um, you see . . . I was thinking veterinarian . . ."

"That's great," said the teacher.

"Or rancher," I continued. "Or cop. But then I saw this TV show on astronauts . . ."

Mr. Manju's smile faded. "You haven't chosen anything, have you?"

I shrugged.

"Hector, you've only got four days left, and this is a big part of your grade. For gosh sakes, son, pick something!"

I nodded, eyes on the floor. "Sure, no problem."

But it *was* a problem.

On the playground at recess, Zeke was full of

suggestions. "Think of all the interesting people we've met lately. Report on one of *their* jobs."

"What, government spy?" I said. "Or evil world-taking-over guy?"

Just then, Stephanie showed up. "Want to go check on our undercover cat?"

"Anything but talk about my report," I said.

But when we reached the hallway outside Mr. Wheener's office, Fitz was nowhere in sight.

"Where is he?" Steph asked.

"He's a cat," I said, looking in the bushes. "He could be anywhere."

"Here, Fitzie-witzie!" Zeke called softly. "Here, you furry meatloaf."

We cruised past the office, but the door was shut. It was covered with flyers for bake sales and book fairs. And a small black poster that read UNDERCHUNDER IS COMING! in green letters.

Steph put her ear to the door. "Fitz!" she hissed.

Zeke's eyes grew big. "Ooh, what if Mr. Wheener caught him snooping and captured him?"

"Think, genius," said Stephanie. "He's a cat. How can anyone tell he's snooping?"

I smirked. "Uh, because his eyes are open?"

A boot scuffed behind us on the cement. "Looking for someone?" said a raspy voice.

We turned. A shaggy-haired janitor stood before us with an orange cat tucked under his arm.

"Reer row," said Fitz.

"Hello, kiddies," said Mr. Wheener.

Double Threat

I gulped. "Uh, hi, Mr. Wheener."

"It's pronounced *Veener*," he said. "You kids never learn."

The janitor's eyes were dirt brown and his teeth were corn yellow. He looked us over like we were candy wrappers on the playground.

"What—uh, what are you doing with my cat?" I squeaked.

"This your cat?" He scratched Fitz between the ears.

Fitz closed his eyes in pleasure. The traitor.

"He wasn't spying or anything," Zeke blurted.

"Spying?" Mr. Wheener raised an eyebrow.

Steph elbowed Zeke. "What my dumb brother means is, cats snoop around where they shouldn't, but they don't mean any harm."

"Cats should be careful," said the janitor. He stepped closer. "They stick their nose in something dangerous, they might lose it."

Fitz struggled in his grip.

"We'll make sure he doesn't bother you again," I said.

Mr. Wheener smiled faintly. "Good idea. After all, what did curiosity kill?"

I gulped again. "The, uh, cat?" I said, reaching for Fitz.

The janitor handed him over. "Smart boy."

He unlocked his door. As casually as possible, we strolled down the hall until we heard it shut. Then we ran onto the grass.

"*Yeesh*, that guy is creepy!" said Zeke.

I held Fitz tight. "Are you all right, buddy?"

He wriggled in my arms, so I put him down.

All three of us squatted beside Fitz.

"So?" said Zeke eagerly. "Where's the Brush? Did Mr. Wheener hide it somewhere? What's he planning?"

Fitz gave him a look, the same one *I* give Zeke sometimes. "*Reeow row.*"

"Let me translate," I said. "He says, 'I can't speak English up here, mouse brain.'"

I could swear Fitz smiled at that.

"But you can nod yes or no, right?" said Steph.

Fitz nodded.

"So let's only ask him yes-or-no questions," I said.

"Brilliant," said Zeke.

Fitz yawned and stretched.

I stroked his back. "So, Spy Cat, did you see the Brush of Wisdom in his office?"

The cat shook his head.

"Did Mr. Wheener talk to anyone about it?" Steph asked.

"*Mrrow.*" Fitz nodded.

"Who?" said Zeke.

Fitz stared at him with extra attitude. Then he held up one paw, tapped it twice on the other paw, and looked up expectantly.

"Huh?" I said.

He repeated the move.

Zeke laughed. "It's almost like he's doing charades."

"*Mreeer!*" Fitz clapped one paw to his nose and nodded.

"Ooh, I like charades!" said Steph. "Okay, um . . . one word, two syllables."

Fitz tapped his paw once and held it up to his ear.

"First syllable," I said. "Sounds like . . ."

Fitz cocked his head like he was listening to something and shook a paw in the air back and forth.

"Um . . . sounds like *flies*?" said Steph. "Uh, *swing*?"

Fitz shook his head no. Just then the class bell rang.

Brrrrring!

He jumped at the sound. *"Rauw rauw reer!"*

"Bell?" said Zeke. "Sounds like *bell*?"

Fitz nodded.

"Let's see," I said. "Tell, fell, well, rell, mell—"

Fitz batted my leg with a paw.

"It's *mell*," said Steph. "Okay, second syllable . . . ?"

My cat stared past us and pointed stiffly.

"Sounds like *point*?" said Zeke. "Mell-point?"

Fitz rolled his eyes. He pointed again, more urgently.

"Mell-jab?" I said.

"Mell-paw?" said Steph.

44

A shadow fell over us. "The name's Melvin," said the bully. "And I know *everything*."

Yikes!

We scrambled to our feet. "You!" I said. "What were you doing in Underwhere?"

Melvin frowned. "I wear 'em every day, dork brain."

"No, the *world* you went to," said Steph. "Down below?"

"Oh, that," said the bully. "You call it *underwear*? That's dumb."

"It's Under*where*." Zeke's jaw tightened. "And you better not, uh, go back."

"Ooh, you got me shaking, runt!" Melvin faked a punch.

Zeke flinched. I wanted to do something but couldn't decide what.

Steph drew herself up. "If you hurt our friends, the Undies . . ."

"Your friends are *undies*?" Melvin's face twisted in a grin. "What does that make your brother, a stinky sweat sock? Haw-haw!"

I spoke up. "She's talking about the people in Underwhere."

"Oh, *them*," said Melvin. He puffed out his chest. "They like me."

"What?" I said, trying to picture a universe where anyone liked Melvin.

He scratched himself. "Yeah, I gave that General Rumblesomething what he wanted. And he said I showed promise! Smart dude."

I bit my lip. "General Rumbletookus?" *Double yikes.*

Steph's eyes narrowed. "He's a bad man, Melvin. You should stay away from him—in fact, stay out of Underwhere."

Melvin looked from one of us to the other.

"Oh, I get it," he said.

"Good," said Zeke, relieved.

"You want to hog the place to yourself."

"No," said Steph. "We—"

"Tough noogies." Melvin sneered. "That Undie-land is brutal cool, and I'm gonna keep on visit-ing."

He turned away.

Curiosity got the better of me. "What did you give the general?" I asked.

The bully smirked over his shoulder. "It's a secret, dweeb face." He stomped off, chuckling.

I scratched my head. "Secrets from Melvin? That can't be good."

Zeke frowned and Steph bit her lip.

Fitz just *mrrowed*. I knew how he felt.

CHAPTER
5

What Would a Hero Do?

The rest of the day didn't get any better. During quiet work time, I researched two more jobs: fireboat captain and bounty hunter. But I couldn't make up my mind about either of them.

We didn't spot Mr. Wheener at lunch (not that we tried very hard). And we weren't able to learn anything else about Melvin's plans.

I puzzled all afternoon. What would a hero do? If we wanted to recover the Brush of Wisdom, drastic measures were needed. We had to look and look . . .

But my thoughts kept coming back to Pegasus. That poor horse—cursed to always have to help people. Maybe if we could break his curse, he'd give us a hand in finding the Brush.

And it'd sure be cool to fly around on his back again . . .

I shook my head. No wonder I was a sidekick. I couldn't focus.

After school, we searched for our spy cat to see what he'd learned. But Fitz was nowhere to be found.

"Maybe he's at home," I said.

"Spying on some tuna fish?" said Zeke.

But he wasn't there, either. Steph, Zeke, and I settled into their living room to talk things over as we waited for Fitz to turn up.

You can't rush a cat.

I sprawled on the couch. "I've been thinking," I said.

"Careful," said Zeke. "It's tricky your first time out."

"Ha, ha. Seriously, how do we break Pegasus's curse?"

"Why?" asked Stephanie.

"Well, for one thing, he'd be a good friend to have," I said.

Zeke shrugged. "Um, okay. But shouldn't we be looking for the Brush?"

"Hector's right," said Stephanie. "That poor horse—we should do something."

"So," I said.

"So," said Zeke.

"How do you break a curse?"

Steph brightened. "A kiss?"

"*Gross*," said Zeke and I together.

"Well, it worked for Sleeping Beauty," she said.

I stood and paced. "Think. How else do you reverse curses? Eating something? Um . . ."

"Breaking something?" said Zeke.

"Let's grab supplies from your closet," I said, leading the way into his bedroom. Zeke and I loaded various helpful-looking things into my book bag.

I eyed his Junior Magic-Maker kit. "Wish we knew what would really work."

Steph leaned in the doorway. "Why don't we just look it up in the Book of Booty?"

I grinned. "Well, sure, if you want to do it the *easy* way . . ."

We trooped into the living room and crowded around Steph, who opened the book on her lap. A faint whiff of rotten eggs rose from it. (The book, not her lap.) (I think.)

The yellowed pages turned stiffly. "Let's see," she said. "'Rain of Newts' . . . 'Death Monkeys' . . . 'Lost Prince' . . . blah, blah, blah . . ."

"Ooh, there!" My finger landed on a drawing of a horse wearing a bridle that looked a lot like a pair of tighty-whities.

"What's it say?" said Zeke.

Steph read aloud:

When through the air the lizards rise
And Flyboy comes to claim the prize,
The whitest horse with wings outspread,
Wears holy fleece upon—

Just then, the cat door in the kitchen went *fwup-fwup*. A streak of orangey fur flew into the living room and leaped onto the open book.

"*Wurr mir reow reow, reer row murrr,*" said Fitz. He was talking a blue streak. His tail was twitching like mad.

"*There* you are!" I said.

"Uh, Hector," said Steph, "is something wrong with him?"

I shrugged. "Aside from the usual? We'll have to visit Underwhere to find out."

"Then what are we waiting for?" said Zeke.

CHAPTER 6

SO WHAT'S THE FUSS, KITTY?

ONE MOMENT. CLEANLINESS IS NEXT TO—

FITZIE!

ALL RIGHT. BIG BOY WAS HANGING AROUND BLEACH MAN'S OFFICE.

BIG BOY?

HE MEANS MELVIN.

BLEACH SAID BIG BOY WAS EYEING THAT BRUSH.

THE *BRUSH* OF *WISDOM?*

AND THEN LATER, IT WAS MISSING.

HUH? I DON'T GET IT.

IN SMALL WORDS? BIG BOY STEAL *BRUSH.* TAKE IT DOWN HERE.

GOOD THINKING, FITZIE!

I DON'T WANT TO SOUND UNGRATEFUL, BUT... WHY ARE YOU SO HELPFUL?

AND ANOTHER...

SSPSSHHH!

OH, WELL. AT LEAST I HAD FUN.

UNTIL...

ANY MORE IDEAS?

JUST ONE. BUT IT'S TOO DUMB TO TRY.

IT CAN'T BE ANY DUMBER THAN YOUR OTHER IDEAS.

WOOSH

HAHAH HAHAHAH HAHAH!

THE HOLY FLEECIES?

GO AHEAD, HECTOR. BUT BE BRIEF!

BY THE POWER VESTED IN ME BY, UM, NOBODY... I DECLARE YOU *ROYAL HORSE* OF UNDERWHERE!

OH MAN. TOO FUNNY, FLYBOY!

STOP- HEE, HEE- TEASING HIM.

BZZZZ ZWITCH!

UH, PEGASUS?

WOOSH

THERE GOES YOUR RIDE.

NEVER MIND HIM. YOU DID A GOOD THING.

NOW HOW WILL WE FIND THE BRUSH?

ISN'T THAT ALF AND WHITEY?

MAYBE THEY'LL KNOW.

WHAT NEWS, YOUR LOST 'IGHNESSES?

THE ZOMBIES ARE ON WHEELS.

WE HAVEN'T FOUND THE BRUSH.

AND I'M HUNGRY.

MAYBE WE CAN 'ELP WITH ONE PROBLEM.

OUR SPIES FOUND THE BRUSH.

THAT'S GREAT, ALF!

NO IT ISN'T.

SOME UPLANDER BOY 'AD IT. MARVIN?

MELVIN! WE CAN STEAL IT FROM HIM.

THAT'S GREAT!

NO IT ISN'T. 'E DOESN'T 'AVE IT ANYMORE.

THEN WHO DOES?

GENERAL RUMBLETOOKUS.

THAT'S... NOT SO GREAT.

AND 'E'S LOCKED IT IN AN 'IGH TOWER, GUARDED BY THUNDER LIZARDS AND FLAPPY LIZARDS.

A HIGH TOWER? HMM..

AT TIMES LIKE THESE, A *FLYING HORSE* WOULD COME IN HANDY.

HEH.

LET'S CHECK IT OUT. MAYBE WE DON'T NEED PEGASUS.

WE'LL HAVE TO WORK ON IT *TOMORROW.*

WHY'S THAT, PRINCESS?

IT'S ALMOST OUR CURFEW.

DARN. IT'S HARD, SAVING THE WORLD BETWEEN SCHOOL AND DINNERTIME.

A Little Alla-Kazaam

By the time we got back to Zeke and Stephanie's house, it was past sunset. Yellow light shone from the front windows.

A loud voice carried from inside the house. "Are those the little trolltags who promised to clean up this kitchen?"

"Uh, this is where I get off," I said, hanging back. "I've heard enough yelling this week."

Zeke muttered, "To tell you the truth, me too."

Steph smirked and led the way up the front steps.

As I headed down the sidewalk, I could already

hear Caitlyn's motor revving up. "Let me guess—your bike got a flat, your elephant died, and you had to hitchhike all the way back from East Obnoxioustan. If you zimwats had half a . . ."

I shook my head. My Grandma Sanchez could be strict sometimes, but for sheer sound volume, nothing compares to the wrath of a college student.

After dinner, I tidied up and got as far as the door.

"Homework?" asked my grandma.

"Done," I said.

"Dishes?"

"Cleaned."

"What about that career project?" she said.

I winced. "Uh, I'm almost there." And that was true—if *almost there* meant "haven't started yet."

Grandma frowned. "Listen, *mi hijito*. Life doesn't wait for you to make up your mind."

"I'm on it, *abuela*. Honest." Grandma always softens up when I use Spanish.

"*Hmph!*" she snorted. But she waved her hand. "Go."

Five minutes later, I was brainstorming with Zeke and Stephanie in their TV room. Caitlyn was somewhere in the back of the house, wearing out her cell phone.

Steph pulled out the Book of Booty. "Let's see if there's anything in here about towers or—"

Rat-a-tat-tat! A knock interrupted her.

"Who could that be?" Zeke asked.

"Probably some friend of Caitlyn's," said Steph. She got up and went to the door.

Caitlyn wandered in from the back room, still gabbing on her phone.

But when Steph opened up, it wasn't Caitlyn's friend, or anyone we knew.

"Good evening, magic lovers!" said a man in black. "I am . . . the Uncanny Underchunder!" He reached into his ear, pulled out a bouquet of roses, and gave it to Caitlyn.

Two women in spangly tights behind him squealed, "Ooh!"

"Magic," whispered Zeke. We moved closer. "I *love* magic."

"May we come in?" asked the magician.

Caitlyn stepped forward. "Laters," she said into her phone.

"Eh?" said Underchunder.

She flipped her cell phone shut and took the flowers. "I've heard of you." Caitlyn looked him up and down. "You're, like, this big whoop-di-walla magician who's gonna do some big whoop-di-dee show next week."

"My fame precedes me," he said, his round face beaming.

"Don't get all, like, Oz-headed," said Caitlyn, sniffing the roses in spite of herself. "I've just *barely* heard of you. What do you want?"

Underchunder strutted stiffly into the room. "I am, as you say, staging a magical extravaganza on Tuesday. And I've chosen several lucky families in your neighborhood for sneak previews!"

His assistants—or whatever they were—burst into applause.

"Thank you. You're too kind," said the magician. "And now, let the enchantment begin!"

As one helper closed the door, Fitz scooted into the room. The other assistant set up a small card table while Underchunder plucked a gold coin from Caitlyn's nostril.

It didn't surprise me. Personally, I think she's got much worse stuff up there.

Stephanie muttered, "He looks *so* familiar. You don't think he could be . . ."

"The UnderLord?" I whispered. "Nah, see how tall he is?"

It was true. This guy was medium height, while the evil UnderLord had actually been shorter than Zeke. (And that's saying something.)

"He's dressed in black," Zeke whispered. "Fitz said Mr. Wheener met a man in black . . ."

"Take your seats, my friends," said the magician. "For my first trick, I will require some ordinary reading material."

Zeke picked up a magazine. "Is this ordinary enough?"

The blond assistant lady carried it to Underchunder. "Observe," he said, passing a hand above and below the magazine. "No strings attached. Nothing inside but pages and perfume ads." He fanned it open, then closed it again.

Fitz sat nearby. Tail twitching, he cut his eyes from me to the magician and back.

"*Mrrrr*," he said. "*Murr reer.*"

Underchunder adjusted his top hat, smiled, and waved his hand three times. "*Alla . . . kaz-ibba . . . kazaam*!"

We stared at the magazine. Nothing had changed.

"Some trick," said Caitlyn.

The magician held up a finger. "But wait." He opened the magazine, and three white doves flew out!

"Wow!" Zeke cried. Everyone clapped.

Fitz followed the birds with interest. After they left by an open window, he padded over to Underchunder and rubbed up against his legs.

"Yes, uh, lovely pet," he said. "Will someone take this cat?"

"Fitzie!" I called. He looked up at Underchunder, then over at me, puzzled. I went and picked him up. (The cat, not the magician.)

"Mer-wowr?" said Fitz.

I set him down on the floor beside the couch.

"Now for my next trick," said Underchunder. "I'll need a common household item from the er, little magicians' room."

"*Reer owr meer MEER*," said Fitz insistently. "*Murr mau.*"

"Perhaps a brush, some paper?" said Underchunder. "Or a spare thro—uh, potty?"

Chomp! Fitz bit my leg.

"Yow!" I cried. "What's *wrong* with you?"

He dodged my grab and scooted away from the couch. "*Rauw rauw REEER.*"

"Well," said Caitlyn doubtfully. "Our brush is, like, maximally skranky, but we've got mucho-mucho T.P. I'll snag some."

She got up and left the room.

Fitz scampered over to Underchunder. "*Meeer!*" he cried, and he sank his teeth into the man's leg.

"Fitz, *no!*" I jumped up.

But Underchunder just looked at us blankly. "Why all the hullabaloo?"

"Your, uh . . ." said Steph, rising.

Zeke stood. "Your leg," he said, "has a cat on it."

The magician glanced down and noticed Fitz. "Off!" Underchunder shook his leg and swayed.

The lady assistants fluttered about, trying to keep their boss from falling.

My own leg was throbbing from Fitz's bite. But this guy hadn't said *boo* when Fitz chomped him.

Strange.

Steph noticed it, too. "He doesn't even feel it," she whispered.

Fitz growled low in his throat, doing his mini-tiger impression. Underchunder shook his leg again and staggered, off balance.

The ladies squealed.

Then, three things happened almost at once.

Fitz finally let go.

The magician fell on his butt.

And his legs broke off.

CHAPTER 8

Bully Dozer

We stared, openmouthed.

Caitlyn rushed into the room. "Omigod, I'm, like, sooo sorry. I'm gonna have that cat zelched, quicker than—" She stopped short. "*Eew*, your legs!"

Underchunder examined his legs, both bent at an unnatural angle. "Oh, they're, uh—how you say?—plastic." He climbed to his feet without them and stood a full foot and a half shorter. Shorter than Zeke, in fact.

Hmm . . . round-faced, short, interested in thrones?

I looked over at Steph and Zeke, and saw it in their eyes.

"I know that melon head," said Zeke. "It's the Under—"

With a glance at Caitlyn, Steph cut him off. "Underchunder! We've had enough of your tricks."

"Yeah." I crossed my arms. "Why don't you do a vanishing act?"

"Don't be rude, runts," said Caitlyn. "Just because he's got fake drumsticks . . ."

"*Mwwwrr,*" growled Fitz from the corner.

The fake Underchunder opened his mouth, began to speak, and then thought better of it.

"Come, ladies," he said to his assistants. "A little leg repair is in order." The magician drew four tickets from his sleeve and handed them to Caitlyn.

"My sneak preview didn't go exactly as

planned," he said, with a sharp look at us. "I hope you'll accept this as an apology."

Caitlyn's eyes grew round. "Free tickets to your show on Tuesday? Flavorful! Totally Tuckahoe way to express your sorry-ness!"

(I've got to say, half the time, I have no idea what Caitlyn's saying.)

The magician's helpers gathered up his props and fake legs and hustled out the door. Underchunder followed, tripping on his pants legs like a three-year-old in his daddy's trousers.

At the door, he turned. "This isn't the final act. I'll see *you* later, kiddies."

"Not if we see you first," I replied. Not the most original thing, maybe, but it had to be said.

The door closed. Caitlyn whipped out her cell phone. "Britney is gonna totally plork when I, like, tell her what just happened." She pranced away.

Zeke slumped on the couch. "And he seemed like such a *nice* magician."

At lunch the next day, we took risky measures. (And I don't mean trying the Chef's Surprise.)

First, we called the spies, who had given us their business card at an earlier meeting. We told them about the Uncanny Underchunder, hoping that they'd trip up his evil plans. (Or that *he'd* trip up *theirs*.)

Second, we worked on a solution to the Melvin problem.

"If we're going to make any headway down in Underwhere," said Steph, as we left the pay phones, "we've got to keep Melvin up *here*."

"Agreed," said Zeke.

"Fine with me," I said. "Any ideas?"

As usual, I couldn't make up my mind about our choices, but Steph pushed her plan through.

Not surprisingly, it involved possible bodily harm to Zeke and me.

Steph went off to handle her side of things while Zeke and I waited in the hall. "Tell me again why *we* have to do this part?" he asked.

"Because *you're* Melvin's favorite target," I said. (What I didn't say was, I wasn't sure I could pull it off on my own. It's scary sometimes, playing hero.)

"Right," said Zeke. His smile was wobbly.

Soon we spotted kids with scared and unhappy faces—which meant Melvin was nearby. He saw us and began terrorizing his way in our direction. As the bully drew closer, my stomach flip-flopped.

Showtime.

"Remember, act natural," I whispered.

"No problem," said Zeke. "Naturally I'm scared out of my mind."

We stood waiting for Melvin to come within earshot.

"Now!" hissed Zeke.

I cleared my throat. "Yeah," I said loudly, "Melvin's so dumb, he, um, flunked recess."

From the corner of my eye, I saw the bully stop dead, mouth open. It took everything I had not to turn and look at him.

Zeke faked a laugh. "Melvin's so, uh, dumb, he got fired from the M&M's factory for throwing out the W's."

"Hey!" Melvin growled, stomping up to us.

Our plan was working!

He planted his fists on his hips. "Is that the best you got? *Bo-ring.*"

Our plan *wasn't* working. We ignored him and tried harder.

"Melvin's momma is so ugly, they're going to move Halloween to her birthday," Zeke said.

Yikes. Zeke had crossed the line.

"No mommas," snarled Melvin.

"Your turn," Zeke hissed at me. But my throat

had closed up.

Zeke's voice shook, but he kept on going. "Melvin's momma is so fat, she walked into the Gap and filled it."

"No *mommas*," growled Melvin, his face turning red.

I felt a little sorry for him, but I could only gape like a goldfish.

"Melvin's momma is so fat," said Zeke, "she sat on a quarter and a booger popped out of George Washington's nose!"

"I said, *no mommas*!" Melvin cried. He dove at Zeke, snatching his T-shirt in both hands and shaking him. "You! *You!*"

I wanted to stop Melvin, but I didn't want to wreck our plan. What to do?

And where was Stephanie?

Melvin grabbed Zeke by the throat and held him high. "I'm gonna . . . !"

Finally Steph showed up, deep in conversation

with our principal, Ms. Johnson. She saw Zeke and gasped.

"Melvin!" shouted the principal. "Put that boy down!"

The bully released Zeke, who slumped to the ground.

"But he—" Melvin said.

"There's *no* excuse for physical violence," said Ms. Johnson. "Come with me, young man. You're getting a week of detention."

The principal dragged Melvin up the hallway. He argued his case, but Ms. Johnson didn't miss a step.

Steph and I dusted off Zeke. "That," I said, "was either the bravest or the stupidest thing I've ever seen."

He smiled shakily. "The old 'yo' mama' joke. Always good for a grin."

* * *

To tell the truth, I was a bit jealous of Zeke's bravery. Once again, he was the hero and I was just the sidekick. A little like Melvin's friend Darryl, but nicer.

Back in class, Mr. Manju didn't help my mood. Moments before the last bell rang, he announced, "Your career reports are due the day after tomorrow. And I had better see some real work from *some* of you."

He looked right at me. I knew without another word that it was time to get cracking on that report.

And I meant to—just as soon as I could make up my mind.

Scepter Protector

That evening was not the most cheerful time I've ever spent at Zeke and Stephanie's house. We sat around the TV room, trying to think of ways to rescue the Brush from the Tower of Dino Death.

"Balloons?" I said. "With enough of them, we could float . . ."

"Right into the pterodactyls' jaws," said Steph.

We fell silent.

"Ooh, a catapult!" said Zeke. "We could launch ourselves—"

"Splat into the wall," I said.

"Maybe a huge pair of stilts?" Stephanie said, then sighed. "Nah."

I put my chin in my hands. If only I hadn't freed Pegasus . . .

The ringing phone interrupted my thoughts.

Zeke picked it up. "Yeah?"

He frowned and leaned forward. "What? Slow down." Zeke glanced up and whispered, "Dr. Prufrock."

Steph and I crowded close, and Zeke turned the receiver so we could hear.

" . . . from Amelia," Dr. Prufrock was saying. "She's got the third artifact, the er, Scepter."

"She *does*?" said Stephanie.

Zeke's smile answered my own. Maybe things were looking up!

"But she just called and said she heard suspicious noises," said Dr. Prufrock. "I'm afraid someone's trying to steal it."

"What'll we do?" I said.

I should mention, Dr. J. Robert Prufrock was a bold explorer and an old friend of Zeke's great-aunt Zenobia, who had been to Underwhere and back.

"Come with me," he said. "There's, er, strength in numbers."

Dr. Prufrock was also a major scaredy-cat.

Steph bit her lip. "I don't think Caitlyn will let us out of the house."

"Please?" said the old man. "See you in ten minutes. You're my only hope."

Zeke hung up the phone. "Hey, so we can't get the Brush. At least we have a shot at the Scepter!"

Steph snorted. "Don't be too sure. Caitlyn will never go for it."

But strangely enough she did. Caitlyn bustled into the TV room and told us all to clear out so she could watch *So You Want to Be a Spoiled Brat?*

We said okay, and could we clear out with Great-aunt Zenobia's friend?

"Fine. But you drizzlewits better be back by the time this show is over," said Caitlyn, settling in with her popcorn. "Or I'll toast you like croutons."

We swore to be back in an hour and hustled out the door.

After waiting in the cold for five minutes, we heard a sputtering and backfiring down the block. Dr. Prufrock's dented gray car was older than prehistoric dirt. It gasped to the curb.

"Hurry, children!" boomed Dr. Prufrock. "Great Milk of Minerva, we haven't much time!"

We piled into the car, and it puttered down the street. We could have *walked* there faster.

"I thought you said this was an emergency," I said.

Dr. Prufrock gripped the steering wheel tightly.

"It is. But one cannot ignore traffic laws. That way lies anarchy."

To pass the time, I brought him up to date on Underwhere, mentioning the missing Brush and my ride on Pegasus.

"You like to fly, eh?" he said. "Maybe you could be a flyboy, like those World War I aces."

Zeke looked over at me and twirled a finger by his ear, in the universal 'He's a loony' sign. I nodded, but I wasn't so sure.

A painfully long drive later, Dr. Prufrock arrived at a small, pretty house. It was lit up like a birthday cake, and a loud barking came from inside.

"Here we are," said Dr. Prufrock. He made no move to get out.

Stephanie opened the front door. "So . . . ?"

"Let's go," said Zeke, bouncing out of the back door. Steph and I followed, and the doctor brought up the rear. We passed a half-burned wooden mailbox that was still smoking.

By the front door, the barking was really loud. "What's she got?" I said. "A Great Dane?"

"Or a so-so Doberman?" said Zeke.

Steph knocked. We waited.

Woof, woof, woof! The barking went on.

"Down, Fang! Down!" said a high, fluty voice.

A spy hole opened in the door and a blue eye peered out. "Who's that?"

From behind us, Dr. Prufrock said, "It's J. Robert, with three friends of Zenobia. Are we, er, too late?"

The spy hole closed. Three locks snapped. The door opened wide.

"Too *late*?" snapped a round old lady in black combat boots. "You're too *early*. Come back just before the *next* time someone steals a magical artifact."

She glared at us. The barking was almost deaf-ening.

I checked the hallway behind her. "Uh, shouldn't

you call off your dog?"

"My what? Oh," said Amelia. She turned to the wall and flicked a switch.

Wooof, woooo . . . The barking wound down.

"What happened?" asked Stephanie.

Amelia patted her fluffy, white old-lady hair. I noticed it had two purple streaks. "Two men robbed my house."

"Er, are they still around?" Dr. Prufrock scanned the front yard.

"No, J," said Amelia. "They lured me outside, and then they slipped into the house, stole the Scepter, and made their escape."

"By Apollo's flameproof booties, Amelia, how could you let yourself be tricked?" the doctor asked.

Amelia put her hands on her round hips. "They set my mailbox on fire."

"Ah."

A thought struck me. "What did these men look like? Did you see them?".

Amelia shook her head no. "But they wore black suits and cheap wigs."

Steph's eyes met mine. "The agents!" we said.

"You *know* these people?" said Amelia.

"Hush," said Zeke.

Amelia frowned. "You watch your mouth, young man."

"That's H.-U.-S.-H." Stephanie spelled it out. "A government agency."

"They're spies," Zeke said.

"Spies?" Amelia echoed. "What in the wide blue world is going on here?"

"That," I said, "is exactly what *we'd* like to know."

CHAPTER 10

Robo-Spies

At school the next day, I had twice the usual help-ing of confusion in my life. Questions chased around in my head: Why had the spies taken the Scepter? How could we get the Brush back? What was the UnderLord (or as he called him-self, the Uncanny Underchunder) up to?

And, oh yeah, would a meteor please hit the school before I had to do my report?

The school day passed quickly. Unfortunately, it passed without bringing any answers.

On the way home, Zeke and Steph and I dis-cussed our friends from H.U.S.H. (And when I say *friends*, I mean "lowdown, wig-wearing double-crossers.")

"Man, I thought they were good guys," I said.

"Good at what?" said Zeke. "They're not good at anything *I* can see."

"How about lying and stealing?" I said.

Steph narrowed her eyes. "We don't know they're *not* good guys."

"So they stole the Scepter for a noble cause?" said Zeke. "Right. Tell us another fairy tale."

"Okay, Dwarf Boy," she said. "Why do *you* think they took it?"

I held up my hands. "Stop, you two! Why don't we just ask them?"

Zeke and I were waiting on the sidewalk when Steph came out of the house.

"I called them," she said. "They're on their way."

Zeke chucked a rock at a tree. "What did you

promise them—state secrets?"

"What they wanted," said Stephanie. "A magical thingie."

"But we don't have one," I said.

"Oh, yes we do." She held up a magazine. "Underchunder made doves fly from this. If that's not magic, what is?"

Zeke pointed at her. "You, you're scary."

Steph just smiled sweetly.

A few minutes later, the agents' silver car pulled up. We approached the passenger side, and Agent Belly rolled down his window.

"Sweet children," he said, in a strangely blank voice. "You called us?"

Steph gave him a weird look. "We have the magical object you wanted."

"Object good." Agent Mole smiled. It was not a pretty sight.

Handing over the magazine, Steph said, "The

Uncanny Underchunder pulled doves from this."

Belly took it. "Doves good. Underchunder good-er. Wonderful magician." His smile seemed mechanical, his voice flat.

"Magic good," said Mole, in the same blank voice.

Zeke raised his eyebrows at me. I nodded. Something was off. They weren't even angry about our lame "magical object."

I decided to test our luck.

"Say, have you guys heard anything about a funny-looking toilet plunger?" I said. "Some call it a Scepter."

Agent Mole's cheek twitched. "Scepter goo— uh, *Scepter?*"

The spies turned to face each other. "Get Scepter. Bring Scepter. Hide Scepter. Good spies," they droned.

Belly turned back to us. "Don't know 'Scepter.' Why you ask?"

"No reason," I said.

He leaned on the car door. "We need old toilet. You have old toilet?"

The *Throne*! Which even now sat in Zeke and Steph's backyard under a tarp.

"Uh, no," said Zeke.

"Why do you ask?" said Steph.

Agent Belly smiled like a robot. "No reason. Bye-bye, sweet children."

"Pay taxes," said Mole. "Taxes good." And they drove off.

"Weird and weirder," said Stephanie.

Zeke scratched his cheek. "Are you guys thinking what I'm thinking?"

"That Spider-Man should be elected president, and that the fountains at school should run with chocolate milk?" I said.

"Not quite," said Steph. "That we should hide the Throne again, and that we never should have told the spies about Underchunder."

Zeke sighed. "Yup. *That's* what *I'm* thinking."

We moved the funky-looking Throne under some bushes by the back fence and headed off for one more trip to Underwhere.

"Better make this quick," said Steph. "We've got a date tonight."

"Gross," I said. "I thought we were just friends."

"Did you forget Underchunder's magic show? We have to be there."

Zeke nodded. "I never thought I'd say this, but she's right. Who knows what he's up to?"

We hustled into the construction site.

"It's funny," I said, "but I'm not as scared as I should be."

"Why should you be scared?" asked Steph.

I stepped inside the half-built house. "Let's see . . . we're facing sure death and two different kinds of hungry dinosaurs. And we don't even have a plan."

"When you put it that way," said Zeke. "I'm scared enough for both of us."

CHAPTER 11

IS PEGASUS HERE?

SORRY, LUV.

WE TRIED WHISTLIN'. NO SIGN OF 'IM.

THEY'RE ON THE MARCH!

THAT'S IT, THEN. TIME TO GO! UNDIES.... OVER ALL!

'UZZAH....

I DON'T LIKE THEIR CHANCES.

I DON'T LIKE OUR CHANCES.

I THOUGHT PEGASUS MIGHTT HELP US AFTER ALL.

AH, WELL. NICE KNOWING YOU.

SAME HERE. IF I DON'T MAKE IT, YOU CAN HAVE MY TRADING CARDS.

SWEET.

NEIGH!

WHAT'S THAT?

IS IT~?

PEGASUS!

YOU DIDN'T DESERT US!

WHAT KIND OF *STEED* ABANDONS HIS HERO?

ALL RIGHT! LET'S GO GET THAT *BRUSH.*

SORRY. ONLY ONE *HERO* PER HORSE.

LET'S GO!

FWIASSHH!

WOO-HOO!
WAY TO GO,
PEGASUS!

WHEEE!

WHO'S GOT THE BRUSH?

THE FLYBOY OF UNDERWHERE!

'UZZAH!

NOOO! NOT THE FLYBOY!

THE PROPHECY! WE'RE LOST!

RUN AWAAAY!

CHAPTER
12

The Uncanny Underthunder

When we popped out of the hole back into our world, Fitz was pacing up and down. "*Meer, murr mrow row!*"

"Sorry, Fitzie," I said. "No time to go below so we can understand you."

He offered me the same stare of disbelief he gives when I won't feed him a second dinner.

I scooped him up, and we hurried out of the construction site. From the looks of the setting sun, we were running a little late.

"*There* you are!" came Caitlyn's bellow.

From the sound of it, we were running *really* late.

She jammed everyone into her sporty red car, chewing us out left and right. There was no time to stash the Brush, so I brought it along.

Caitlyn's mouth kept moving all the way across town. She was still griping as we left the car in the parking lot and headed for the theater.

"I've never met such a tofu-brained bunch of dorgwollops in my whole life," she said. "If you zimwats are late *one* more time, I swear I'm gonna lock a tracking device on you." She forged ahead toward the theater doors.

"*Mrwwr*," Fitz muttered.

"You said it, Fitzie," I said.

On the theater marquee, a huge sign read UNDERCHUNDER IS HERE! Above the electric green letters, two seriously spooky eyes stared down.

Caitlyn pushed through the crowd and found some seats on the right, not too far back. I put

Fitz and the Brush on my lap.

People milled about, buzzing excitedly.

I noticed several kids from my class, which was nice, and Melvin and Mr. Wheener, which was not. "We've got company," I said.

Steph and Zeke followed my gaze.

Melvin saw us watching. His face clouded over, and he pointed a finger, then pretended to choke it to death.

"Looks like detention doesn't agree with Melvin," I said.

Zeke sighed. "I am *so* dead."

The lights blinked off and on, and everyone took their seats. The theater slowly went dark. Dramatic music pumped up.

A voice so low it made your seat quiver said, "Prepare yourself to enter . . . the world of illusion. Ladies and gentlemen, please welcome . . . the Uncanny Underchunder!"

A spotlight hit the red curtains. *Poomf!* Sparks showered, blue smoke billowed, and suddenly Underchunder stood on the stage.

The audience went "Oooh!" and clapped wildly.

Zeke leaned over. "You gotta admit, *that* was pretty cool."

"For an evil warlord," I said.

"I *love* magic." Zeke grinned.

Steph, sitting on my other side, went, "Hmph."

Standing tall on his stilt legs, Underchunder raised his hands for quiet. "We are about to leave the known world and enter the realm of the uncanny. A land where *anything* can happen."

He frowned and rubbed his stomach in a fake-y way. "Eh, what's this?" The magician coughed, and then reached into his mouth.

Out came some purple fabric. He pulled, faster and faster, and an ever-lengthening chain of cloth spilled from his mouth. As I looked closer, I realized . . .

"It's undies!" said Zeke.

It was true. Underchunder tugged until a huge chain of silk undies in all colors lay piled on the stage. The audience laughed and applauded.

With a flourish, the magician plucked a wand from his sleeve and struck the pile of cloth. *"Alla-kazammo, bibbity-BOW!"*

It rose into the air and fanned out into an undie rainbow. With another swipe of the wand, Underchunder turned it into a *real* rainbow, which grew fainter and fainter until it faded altogether.

"Aaaahh!" The crowd cheered.

Underchunder clapped twice. The spies from H.U.S.H., still in their black suits and wigs, wheeled a strange contraption onto the stage. A man-sized disk painted with a spiral was mounted in a fancy silver frame.

"What are *they* doing?" muttered Stephanie.

I shrugged.

"Observe," said the magician, "the All-Seeing Eye of Ungawa. Keep your gaze fixed on the center of the wheel."

Moving like sleepwalkers, agents Belly and Mole braced the frame from either side. Underchunder reached up and grabbed the disk, then pulled down sharply. The circle spun. Its painted lines spiraled inward.

Like a magnet, it drew my attention.

"Yes, that's right," said Underchunder. "You're watching the wheel, nothing else. You find yourself going deeper . . . deeper inside . . . relaxing *so* deeply . . ."

I was sinking into the center of the disk. So calm, so peaceful . . .

Someone's claws dug into my leg.

"Ow!" I glanced down. "Fitz, that hurt!"

"*Wurrr meer row murr row,*" he said, jerking

his head toward Zeke.

My buddy had gone slack-jawed, staring at the stage. So had Caitlyn and everyone beyond them. I turned the other way. Steph was hypnotized too.

What to do?

This time, I acted without thinking.

I nudged her. "Steph!" No reaction. I pinched her, hard.

"Ouch!" Stephanie snapped out of it. "What'd you do that fo—?" She took in the mesmerized audience. "Oh."

"You're all sinking even deeper," said Underchunder from the stage. "That's right. Let me hear you say, 'Yes, master.'"

"Yes, master," came from a few hundred loose mouths.

"Yeah, master," said Zeke.

I turned to shake him.

Steph stopped me. "Let *me*." She leaned over

and savagely pinched his arm.

"Ow!" Zeke said. "What—"

I cut him off. "*Shh!* Underchunder is hypnotizing everyone. We've got to stop him."

Fitz batted my hand with a paw. I looked down and saw the Brush of Wisdom in his mouth.

"Good thinking, Fitzie." I took it from him. "Let's sneak up there before something *really* bad happens."

Crouching low, we edged past the others in our row and out into the aisle. I checked the stage. Underchunder had turned his back and was reaching into a shiny blue sack.

"Go!" I hissed.

The four of us scooted up the side aisle. We were just climbing the stairs to the stage when the magician spoke again.

"Everyone repeat after me: 'The UnderLord is my ruler.'"

"The UnderLord is my ruler," said the crowd.

I shot a worried glance at my friends. This was worse than I thought.

As we crept closer, the magician drew something from the bag. It was the length of a man's forearm, glittering with gold, and capped by a jeweled cup. It looked like the Pope's best bathroom plunger.

"The Scepter!" whispered Steph.

Zeke blinked. "What's he going to do with that?"

"I don't know," I said. "But I bet he's not here to fix their toilets."

CHAPTER 13

Toilet Plunger of Death

The Uncanny Underchunder jammed the Scepter onto the back of the spinning disk. It stuck with a loud *chook*. He twirled the handle.

The wheel spun faster.

"Repeat after me," he said. " 'I will obey the UnderLord and keep my undies cottony-fresh.' "

The dazed audience said, "I will obey the UnderLord and keep my undies cottony-fresh."

Just then, we hit the stage and Underchunder noticed us. "You . . . interfering brats!" he cried.

"You . . . interfering brats," the crowd repeated.

The magician signaled the spies. "Agents, stop them!"

"Agents, stop them," said the audience.

Underchunder frowned. "Stop repeating everything I say."

"Stop repeating everything I say."

"I'm not kidding!" snarled the magician.

"I'm not kidding," said the audience.

But I had no time to notice what else they said, because the two spies were marching toward us with arms spread wide.

"Yeesh!" said Zeke.

"Yikes!" I cried.

"*Wurrr,*" said Fitz.

The two big men blocked us from Underchunder.

I froze. How on earth would we get around them?

"Any ideas, Flyboy?" said Steph.

And that's when it hit me. "Zeke, go left. Steph, go right."

"What are *you* going to do?" asked Zeke.

"Pterodactyl move, on three," I said. "One . . . two . . ."

"Sweet children," said Agent Belly.

"Resistance bad," said Mole.

"THREE!" I cried.

Zeke split left and Steph dashed right, drawing the spies apart. I ran up the middle, straight for the phony magician.

Underchunder seemed to have the crowd back under control. He reached for the Scepter's handle and gave it another twist. "And now you will—"

"Stop right there," I said, pointing the Brush at him.

"*Rrrowr*," Fitz snarled.

Underchunder turned to face me. "You and your mangy cat. Give me the Brush, and I'll *only* turn you into zombies."

"You and your mangy cat," the audience repeated. "Give me the Brush, and I'll *only* turn you into zombies."

Underchunder growled and rolled his eyes.

I gulped. "No way, boxer breath." I raised the Brush like a sword. "En *garde!*"

The magician plucked the Scepter from the wheel. He wielded it with a wicked grin.

Swooosh! He swung. And *whonk!* I blocked.

We slashed at each other with the fancy bathroom accessories. Back and forth we staggered, like in a bad pirate movie. Underchunder was stronger, but unsteady on his stilt legs.

I ducked and dodged a blow. Then I risked a glance at Zeke and Steph. Mole had caught Zeke by the arm, but Steph was still dancing around Belly.

Thonk!

Something hit me, and I saw stars. Under-chunder!

I clapped one hand to my head and held up the Brush to block his next blow. My legs felt all rubbery.

Could I hold him off alone?

Underchunder raised his arm high, then . . .

"*Reeeow!*" An orange streak leaped from the floor.

"*Aiieee!*" cried Underchunder, dropping the Scepter.

"*Aiieee!*" the crowd responded.

The magician spun and swiped at his backside.

Fitz had clamped onto his butt with a kitty death grip of claws and fangs. Underchunder whirled around and around swatting at him, and Fitz's body swung straight out with the g-force.

But he hung on.

"Let goooooo!" the magician bellowed.

"Let goooooo!" the audience repeated.

Out of control, Underchunder teetered this way and that, stumbling toward the hypnotic wheel.

I held my breath.

At the last possible second, Fitz *did* let go. He sailed into the curtains and landed safely.

Underchunder wasn't so lucky.

Ba-TONK! He plowed straight into the magical contraption.

Kitsssssh! The disc shattered, and Underchunder went facedown in the wreckage.

I looked out at the crowd. Everyone was yawning and rubbing their eyes.

"Wuzzat?" said a curly-haired lady in the front row.

"Is the show over?" her friend asked.

People started standing up. "That's *it*?" Caitlyn bellowed. "A bogus underwear rainbow and, like, a broken wheel?"

I turned to check on my friends.

Agents Belly and Mole were blinking and shaking their heads, Zeke and Steph forgotten.

"You know how I said I like magic?" said Zeke.

"Yeah?" I said.

"I don't like magic."

Steph smoothed back her hair. "The Scepter must have some serious powers. Whatever it does, I'm glad he didn't get to use it."

"Except on my head." I checked the stage. "Uh, guys? Where *is* the Scepter?"

"Didn't *you* grab it?" said Zeke.

We searched, but we couldn't find the Scepter. By this time, half the audience had left. Anyone could've taken it, even . . .

"Hey, where's Mr. Wheener?" I asked.

"And Melvin?" said Steph.

Both were missing.

"That can't be good," said Zeke. "But at least

we've still got the Under—"

We turned. But like the slippery rat he was, the Uncanny UnderLord had slipped away.

"*Again?*" Steph said.

"*Wurr meer,*" Fitz said. He was smoothing his whiskers.

I petted him. "Nice butt-biting, Fitzie. You really saved my neck."

Fitz just purred.

Winging It

Hypnotism was on our minds the next day at lunch. Zeke and I talked it over as we tossed the football.

"So those people last night?" he said. "Think they're still under his spell?"

"Beats me," I said. "It was hypnosis interruptus. Plus, they thought he was *Underchunder*, not the UnderLord." I chased Zeke's long pass.

"Hey, at least you stopped him," Zeke called.

I beamed in spite of myself. "Guess I'm not just a sidekick anymore."

He frowned. "*Sidekick?* Whoever said you were a sidekick? That's nuts."

A lump formed in my throat. I didn't know what to say. But Stephanie's arrival saved me. "Hector, don't you have something better to do?"

"Like what?" I threw the ball back to Zeke.

"Isn't your career report due today?"

I shrugged. "Oh, that."

"You should take it more seriously," she said. "It's a big part of your grade, and you haven't even figured out what job to report on."

"As a matter of fact," I said, "I have."

Twenty minutes later, I was standing in front of Mr. Manju's class holding the library book I'd checked out that morning.

"Well, Hector?" he said. "Have you finally chosen your dream career?"

I smiled. "Yes, Mr. Manju." I held up the book. "Flyboy."

The class laughed.

"Flyboy?" he repeated.

"Yeah, that's what they called the first fighter pilots, back in World War I. And I'd like to be a pilot."

I continued, showing photos from the book and describing what it felt like to be in a dogfight. Of course, I didn't mention that my dogfight was with pterodactyls, or that I was riding a winged horse.

Every flyboy is entitled to some secrets.

As my talk went on, I felt a warm glow. Maybe I didn't have the fanciest report in class, maybe I wouldn't get the best grade. But I knew one thing: I had finally made up my mind.

Just as I was finishing, a movement in the back of the room distracted me. I ignored it and kept talking.

And then, there it was again: an orange flash outside the window.

"And that's why I think being a pilot is, uh . . ."

This time I saw it clearly: Fitz, zooming up into the air, silently yowling, and dropping back out of sight.

" . . . A really cool thing. Mr. Manju, may I step outside for a minute?"

He coughed. "Don't you think you should wait for questions?"

"Oh, yeah," I said. "Any questions? No?" I started for the door. "Thanks, you've been a great audience."

"*I* have a question," came Mr. Manju's voice behind me.

Uh-oh. I turned. "Yes?"

My teacher's face wore a dreamy look. "How do you think it feels, flying up there above everything, so free?"

I took a breath and thought about soaring through the skies on Pegasus. "Absolutely amazing," I said. "Beyond words."

With that, I headed for the door and my jumping cat. Something was afoot in Underwhere. And the Flyboy was about to take off again.

Sharpen your claws and get ready
for some feline fury in
the next Underwhere adventure!

A strong, funky odor hit my nostrils—a blend of dog and . . . lizard?

"What th—?" said Garlic Breath. My thoughts exactly.

All the hairs on my back stood up as a strange creature exploded from the bushes. It combined the ugliness of a dog with the scariness of a giant lizard. Three horns jutted from its broad head. A powerful, black-furred body tapered into a scaly tail.

It carried the Scepter in its jaws, and it was headed straight at me!

"*Reeeow!*"

Every backyard tiger knows there's a time to

1

fight and a time to run.

This was the time to run.

I shot across the driveway and up the nearest tree.

"Gurrr*umph!*" the creature growled around the stick in its mouth.

I clung to the lowest branch and looked down.

The humans screamed and scampered about. If they'd had a little cat-sense, they would have joined me.

"Don't let it escape!" cried Onion Breath. He chased the dog-lizard thing, but when it whirled on him, he screamed and fled. "*Aaugh!*"

"It's got the Scepter!" Stephanie shouted. "Stop it!"

Zeke leaped aside as the creature thundered past. "*You* stop it."

Hector crouched, ready to catch the monster. At the last second, the dog-lizard feinted with its

2

horns, and Hector hopped back, landing on his butt in the bushes.

From my perch, I watched the thing power down the sidewalk and push through the fence around a half-built house.

"Don't look now, but it's going into the construction site," I said.

Zeke glanced down the street. "Hey, you guys, it's going into the construction site."

My whiskers twitched. "My, aren't you the clever one."

The boy ignored me.

"Let's go!" cried Stephanie.

The spies seized her and Zeke. "Not so fast," said Onion Breath.

"But, the monster—" said Zeke, struggling.

"Exactly," said Garlic Breath.

Onion Breath loomed over the kids. "Where did you get that thing?"

"Us?" said Stephanie. "It's not *our* doggie-lizard-whatever."

"Likely story," said Garlic Breath.

"She's right," said Zeke. "We don't even know what it is."

My human frowned. "Let's see, it had the head of a triceratops, the body of a Labrador retriever, and the fur of a poodle," he said. "That makes it . . ."

"A labceradle?" said Stephanie.

"A poobradoratops?" said Zeke.

"Nope," said Hector. "A . . . triceradoodle."

I shifted on the branch. "Whatever you call it, it's going to Underwhere."

Everybody ignored me. Tch, *humans*.

Onion Breath growled. "You children had better bring back that tricera-whatsit, and the magical thingamajig, too."

"That's what we're *trying* to do," said Stephanie.

4

"If you'll just let us go," said Zeke.

The two spies looked at each other.

"All right," said Onion Breath. "But if you try to pull a fast one . . ."

"Us?" said Hector. "Never."

In his case, *never* meant *not in the last five minutes.*

Nevertheless, the spies let go, and the children started off.

"Wait," said Hector.

"What?" said Zeke.

My human pointed up at me. "Fitz. We need him to track the Triceradoodle."

"Hector's right," said Stephanie. "It's got a head start."

They gazed up at me. I pretended not to notice and busied myself with cleaning my paws. (Tree climbing is *filthy* work.)

"What do you say, Fitzie?" said Hector.

I shook my head.

"Please?" said Stephanie. "We'll give you a nice piece of tuna for dinner."

My tail twitched. We needed the Scepter, but it would take a lot more than tuna to make *this* cat chase a savage dino dog.

"And that electric blanket you wanted?" said Hector. "All yours."

Aw, wax my whiskers.

I knew I would regret it. I sighed a long sigh— twice the usual length, for maximum effect—and climbed down from the tree. Then I led the way to the half-built house where the portal to Underwhere waited.

A *normal* cat would've stayed up in the tree.

I was well past being a normal cat.